SHADOW OF THE HERO SERIES: NOVELLA 3

VACATION

SEAN E. LUNDGREN

ISBN (paperback): 978-1-959807-02-5
ISBN (ebook): 978-1-959807-03-2

VACATION

IT WAS SUPPOSED TO BE THEIR NIGHT OFF.

Colt winced at the screeching of the jeep's brakes; they sounded like a banshee's cry as the jeep turned into the gym parking lot.

"Really?" muttered Grace, cupping her hands over her ears. In the backseat, Seamus and Murph joined her in covering their ears.

"I'll get those fixed tomorrow . . . I mean later today." Colt checked the clock on the dash. It changed to 03:23 a.m. It'd been a long day, and they needed some rest.

Before everything had happened, and they were sent out, he was going to visit the hospital. But the hospital definitely wouldn't let him visit this late. They were lenient, but not that lenient.

Grace slid out of the jeep before it had completely stopped, slamming the door behind her. She stomped toward the gym door.

As a Vigil team, living in and operating a rundown gym in Hicken, Texas, wasn't the most glorious assignment, but it was their assignment, and it was their job to protect the people from monsters that they didn't even believe existed. Colt did like the perk of having access to training equipment whenever they needed it.

1

Colt put the jeep into park. "Hey Murph, could you get the equipment from the back and bring it inside?" He had to jerk the shifter a few times whenever he wanted to get it into neutral, but besides that and the breaks, she was still a good car. She was what they had and got them where they needed to go; that was all Colt could ask for.

Murph replied with a simple grunt before squeezing out his door—he made the jeep look like a clown car—leaving Seamus alone in the backseat with his head down, the light glinting off his wavy, bright red hair.

"You did great out there, kid!" Colt turned his head so that Seamus could see his smile. "None of us knew that there were going to be that many desert naga." Seamus lifted his chin slightly, his blue eyes meeting Colt's looking for reassurance. Colt nodded. "It's late and we could all use some sleep. We can debrief in the morning." When he saw Seamus crack a smile, Colt opened his door to get out. His legs wobbled for the first few steps. They were sore from sitting for so long and he felt drained after using his abilities in the fight. "Don't forget to drink water," he said to Seamus. After all the fighting and adrenaline, combined with fatigue, it was easy to get dehydrated without noticing.

Colt joined the others at the door and looked down over Grace's head; she viciously rattled and jiggled her key in the gym door lock. Seamus reached his hand out to help her with the door, but Colt caught his arm, gripping the brown sleeve of his hoodie. Colt shook his head; she needed some space. And the last thing *he* needed was another thing for her to complain about. All they had to do was get things cleaned up and he could get some sleep. As much as he didn't want to, he still had the responsibility of opening the gym on time in a few hours.

Actually, he couldn't even remember the last time Grace and Murph had a break. With the recent desert naga outbreak, they'd spent nearly all their free time the last month hunting them down.

Murph stepped up behind them, towering over the rest of the team. His dark skin and hair made him look like a shadow in the security lights, his arms full of their equipment.

"This is great. *Just* great." Grace jiggled the key more furiously. With a grunt, pressing against the door with her shoulder, the door finally clicked and opened. A loud splat of goop dropped from her brown jacket; it streaked down her jean skirt and plopped onto the floor. "*That's it.* I'm taking a shower and going to bed." Grace ran her fingers through her blond hair as they all entered; a look of disgust spread across her face when she pulled her fingers out covered in yellow goop.

"Sorry." Murph sheepishly stepped away from her.

She flicked the yellow goop onto the floor. "You *had* to slice one open right above me, didn't you?" Murph shrugged his shoulders, trying to put down the weapons and bags in his arms. Grace groaned in frustration and glared at Seamus. "Cleaning this seems like your kind of job, *Swabby.*"

"Language," chimed in Colt. He didn't think asking them to show each other respect was too much to ask for, tired or not.

"It's not even a bad word." Grace flicked on the lights and marched to her room above the gym.

"I still don't like it," said Colt.

The light revealed that Colt, Murph, Seamus, and all their equipment in Murph's hands dripped the yellow viscera from the desert naga nest they'd cleared out all over the worn gym floor.

Murph glanced up where Grace had gone and raised his eyebrow at Colt, sliding off his heavy boots. Murph had always been the level headed one of the group, looking to Colt to know when he should try and make peace or to try and help.

"I know, buddy." said Colt. "She'll calm down. It's fine. She's just upset because those are her favorite sneakers and this was supposed to be our night off." He patted Murph on the shoulder. More yellow goop slopped onto the floor: the sound of another victory for the Vigil, defending humanity against the monsters of the world.

Murph set their equipment on the ground, took off his brown hoodie, and slopped it in a lump next to the front door. Then Seamus took his matching hoodie off, adding it to Murph's pile. He looked back at Colt, avoiding eye contact, waiting for his orders. With how high and tense his shoulders were, Seamus reminded Colt of a turtle trying to hide in its shell.

"Probably best if I clean this up." Colt forced a smile for morale. "Don't worry Seamus, I won't force work on you just because you're new." A little tension left Seamus's shoulders.

Murph cleared his throat, locking eyes with Colt.

"Don't worry about Grace, Murph. She'll be fine after she gets a hot shower and some fresh clothes on. Get yourselves cleaned up. I'll get started on things here." Murph nodded in agreement as he wiped some excess yellow gunk off his clothes. Colt chuckled, watching him; it made him think of a kid trying to wipe away their snot after sneezing into their hands. "Murph, I'd take a shower now if I was you; I'm still expecting you up for the morning shift with me."

Murph's eyebrows sunk deep with exhaustion before starting his tired march up to his room.

"Colt, you shouldn't be the one cleaning this up." Seamus brushed the yellow gunk off his gray shirt and jeans. "You need to get some rest too, so you can keep training for the Shinigami Festival."

Colt unbuckled his sword belt, tossing it to the pile Murph had started. He slid his brown leather jacket off and set it down. The chain bracelet on his wrist jingled slightly. "The Shinigami Festival is months away. We've got enough to do here without me trying to rank up. Anyway, if you keep up with your training, you'll be ready for the festival yourself, soon enough."

"Come on Colt," Seamus said. "You took out like half those desert naga yourself. If there's anyone that deserves to rank up, it's you. Besides, if I'd been more focused, I could've stopped that naga before it was on top of Grace. Then Murph wouldn't have had to gut it all over us."

Colt walked to the corner of the gym floor to get a bucket and mop, then started rolling it back toward the door. Seamus was already on all fours scrubbing the floor with a rag, his Vigil chain hanging low from his neck.

Colt noticed that Seamus's chain almost dragged on the ground. He bent to help clean. "Most of us wear our chains around our wrists after graduation. It keeps them out of the way."

"Oh, I've just gotten used to wearing it this way." He took it off his neck and hung it on his wrist. The metal compressed and condensed into a bracelet. Every Vigil received one when they graduated from the academy. Special extra links had to be earned.

"There, that looks better, and it'll keep it out of the way." Colt scrubbed the floor harder. "We all make mistakes, Seamus," said Colt, going back to their previous conversation. "The important thing is to learn from them." He paused; it sounded like there was something outside. The door was slightly ajar.

"Is everything alright?" Seamus's voice raised with concern as Colt stood to see through the doorway.

The lamppost outside the gym flickered a few times before producing a steady stream of light again. Colt couldn't shake the feeling that they were being watched, even though he couldn't see anything in the night.

"Yeah, fine." Colt closed the door quickly. Seamus didn't look up as he scrubbed more aggressively. "This wasn't how I expected your first mission with us to go. But sometimes we have to move when we get information."

"Yeah . . . You shouldn't let Grace talk to you that way."

Colt slopped the yellow goop around with the mop, then wrung it out in the bucket. "Grace is just having an awful night. Normally, she isn't like this. She knows the mission comes before civilian life."

"And I don't think she should fraternize with the beknighted. We might protect them. But we shouldn't lower ourselves to their level."

"Your family doesn't employee benighted, do they?"

"No." Seamus stretched his back, sitting on his knees. "My family only employs mages, or those from mage families. It makes things easier."

"You might find that they aren't much different from us if you took the chance to get to know them." Colt used the edge of his sleeve to wipe the sweat from his forehead. It was dripping from his dark brown hair. He watched the drops of sweat drip to the ground. This was going to take all night. "Hey, aren't you a hydromancer?"

"Yes?"

"I think cleaning this up might be easier with your abilities." Colt motioned to the yellow goop on the ground.

Seamus gave a reluctant nod, then reached his hand out toward the mop bucket. He closed his eyes and moved his fingers together and apart as he lifted his hand in the air. The water rose out of the bucket, separating from the viscera of the desert naga. "My father taught me the value of doing work ourselves, not only relying on magic."

"Good and wise advice. But I think at four in the morning we can make an exception," said Colt.

Seamus chuckled. "I suppose you're right." He scooped up the mess with his water, dropping the viscera into the bucket, then reusing the clean water and collecting more.

"That's more like it." Colt mopped faster, eager to get to bed.

It didn't take long to clean up most of the mess on the floor using this method. As they were finishing the floor, the front door creaked, opening slightly behind them. Colt's hand dropped to his knife. It was probably just some drunk, but he'd seen enough to be cautious. Seamus reached down for his pistol out of their pile of equipment, his eyes focused on the dark entrance.

Colt shook his head at him, waving for Seamus to put his weapon away. "Sorry," Colt called out and continued to mop the floor. There was no reason to panic or get overanxious. "We're closed right now. We open up again in the morning at eight."

"Even for an old friend?" asked a deep, familiar voice.

Colt dropped his mop. His heart calmed, an enormous smile stretching across his face. "Jorah!" Clearing his throat, Colt stood at attention. "Sorry, I mean Grand Dominus."

Jorah pulled the door open, letting himself in. "There is no need to be so formal. I'm here unofficially." He motioned to his rich-brown button-up shirt, a few shades lighter than his own skin, and his blue jeans. "I saw your jeep on my way in. I'd burn that thing and requisition a new one if I were you. How many desert naga did your team find in that nest? The Church reports I read had them at only about six or seven strong."

Not that the Church reports were ever completely accurate. They were built from rumors and gossip. At least, that was Colt's opinion.

"Twenty, sir." Seamus placed his left fist over his heart in salute. "There were twenty desert naga. Sir."

"Mr. Hayes, no need to call me sir. I'm just here visiting a friend," Jorah said to Seamus, clasping his hand on Colt's shoulder. "Relax." Jorah tugged at his own short curly white hair. "*My.* You certainly carry your families' qualities. I've always been jealous of your family's brilliant red hair. Even in my younger years, my hair wasn't anything to brag about."

"You look great for your age." Colt tried to keep a straight face. "And I mean, when you've been around for *over* a century, you shouldn't worry about your appearance anymore."

Jorah grinned wildly. "Now you owe me a drink. Shall we adjourn to your office?"

"Oh yes, right this way. Seamus, do you mind finishing things up in here?"

"Not at all, sir." Seamus stood at attention. "Pleasure to meet you, Grand Dominus."

Jorah carefully stepped around the viscera that was still on the floor, using his black wooden cane to steady himself. "Nice to finally meet you, Mr. Hayes." Jorah, tightening his grip around the large metal icosahedron on the top of his cane and then slowly releasing. "Thank you for doing your duty."

Colt quickened his pace, walking to the breakroom that led to his office. He knew it was a disaster, dishes overflowing out of the sink. He grabbed the trashcan, sweeping the garbage littered over the table into it with his hand, before shoving it in the corner.

As Jorah reached the breakroom, Colt opened the door of the refrigerator next to the sink, saying, "I've got milk, I think. Oh, and a can of soda."

"Water would be great, thank you." Jorah took a seat at the breakroom table.

"Did my father ask you to come out here and checkup on me?" asked Colt, rummaging past half-empty takeout containers trying not to sound annoyed with his father until he found a bottle of water.

Jorah took the bottle of water and sipped it. "He asked me to look in on you when I could, but that's not why I'm here tonight." He motioned to the breakroom door. "Do you mind?"

Colt closed the door and took a seat next to Jorah. "It is a little early in the morning for all the pleasantries. I appreciate you getting to the point."

"What do you know about Sol Levante?" Jorah took a deep breath, waiting for Colt's reply.

"That religious group in South America? Not a lot, just

that they've got some sort of cult following and are calling the world to repentance."

"The Church keeps sending us disturbing reports of strange creatures wherever Sol Levante appears. And then whenever I send teams to investigate, they report back that everything is fine."

"If you are going where I think with this, then no offense, but my team isn't . . . well, they *aren't* . . . I wouldn't call us a good fit for this kind of mission. Murph isn't exactly inconspicuous; Grace is skilled but doesn't have the temperament for reconnaissance; and Seamus has a lot of potential, but he is still very green in the field."

Jorah leaned back in his chair. "*Trust.* Right now, trust is the most important thing to me. Skill might help me find the truth, but I need someone that I can trust to let me know what is really happening now in Colombia."

"You've got the wrong group." Colt shook his head. "We don't know how to work as a team. Tonight, made that *very* obvious. I'm sure there are others you can send that are trustworthy. We're just a small team trying to figure things out. We aren't anything special."

Jorah grinned. "Exactly! I trust you, and no one will think twice about the four of you being down there."

"Sending a team from Texas to Colombia on a mission seems kind of suspicious to me. There are at least a dozen teams that are closer."

Without missing a beat, Jorah reached into his pocket and slid an envelope across the table to Colt. "Not if they think you are out there on vacation." There were four tickets to Colombia in the envelope, along with a thick stack of money and a printed itinerary with hotel information.

"I thought things might be easier if I gave each of you separate rooms."

"Wait, no, I told you my team isn't up for this kind of task." Colt shoved everything back in the envelope, trying not to get frustrated.

"Okay, then look, I don't need your entire team, Colt; I just need you. Let them enjoy some vacation time, you enjoy some too, but if you notice something, let me know. I think they are using an artifact down there, something that they don't understand. It's only a matter of time until they do something wrong, or lose control, and thousands of innocents pay the price."

"I'm still not sure," said Colt, crossing his arms and tried to remember the last time he'd taken an actual break. He knew they weren't ready, but they *could* use a vacation. Reconnaissance wasn't actual work, anyway.

"Whatever you're cooking, Colt," called out Grace, letting herself into the breakroom, "count me in! I've got a minute before I told the girls to pick me up for this morning's bonfire." She was fully dressed up in a short pink party dress and cowboy boots, her hair wrapped in a towel. "I think I finally got all the naga out the *fifth* time I washed my hair." She finally glanced up from her phone toward the table. Her face took on a flush that was quickly turning bright red. "Sir . . . Master. I mean, Grandmaster Jorah. Good evening."

"Ms. Jones, please don't worry. This was an unannounced visit late at night."

"Sorry, the Swabb . . . I mean *Seamus* told me Colt was in here, so I thought he was cooking something up." Her voice trailed off.

"Colts cookin'! Mmmmm." Murph danced over to the breakroom in his sweatshirt and sweatpants. Grace cleared her throat. "I know. I'll get to cleaning after we eat." Stepping through the door and seeing Jorah, Murph turned about as red as Grace.

Colt watched Jorah. This was it: this would show him this team wasn't ready.

"All of you, take a seat," said Jorah. "It sounds like you've had a busy night. Let me whip up something to eat. Please take a seat." He went to their refrigerator. Grace and Murph stood frozen in the doorway. "For now, that was a suggestion. It can quickly turn into an order." Jorah shuffled around a few items in their fridge. "We give all of you a food stipend, correct?"

Colt dropped the envelope on the table, rushing to the refrigerator. "I'll help you out, Jorah. No need for you to overexert yourself."

With a look of disgust at the state of the refrigerator, Jorah closed the door. "Maybe no food tonight, but that shouldn't be a problem. It's too early in the morning, anyway. The four of you seem like you could use some vacation time. How does a beach in Colombia sound?"

Grace beamed, looking at the tickets. "Yes sir, thank you sir." Grace giddily pulled out her phone, texting furiously.

"Thank you, sir," said Murph, standing at attention.

"I recommend you get packing. The plane leaves early in the morning. Don't forget to let Seamus know." Murph and Grace took off like excited children. Jorah gave Colt a wink. Colt sighed and gripped the envelope tightly. "Fine; I'll do it." Jorah had played his hand well.

"I knew you would." Jorah continued in a hushed tone, "And don't worry about . . . *her*. I'll have Phil check in on her while you're away. I trust him." Then, changing back to his normal voice and tone, Jorah continued. "Try to have some fun while you're out there. It's a vacation, after all."

TURQUOISE WATER SHIMMERED, MOUNTING AGAINST THE WHITE SANDS of the beach, the sand a white brushstroke against the canvas of the land before the rich greens of the jungle. Shining brightly from above, the sun was a spotlight showcasing the beauty of the surrounding nature, not a cloud in the sky to take away from the view. Colt reached his arms out as far as he could. The sun hugged him with the embrace of a soft blanket. After two days of nothing happening, no missions, no desert naga, and his nerves were finally settling.

Which was more than he could say for Seamus. Beams of sunlight finally cut through the shade of the tree Seamus was standing under, forcing him to run under a beach umbrella. Colt chuckled, watching Seamus liberally rub sunscreen on his pasty skin again. He did it every hour, like clockwork.

Colt stepped forward with his right leg, keeping his left extended while reaching his arms apart from each other, taking a warrior II pose. He kept his movements slow and controlled; he didn't want to accidentally hit one of the children running around. They were laughing, running up and down the beach, into the water, and splashing around in the shallows with parents keeping a watchful eye. As Colt moved through his yoga poses, one kid dashed past

Murph's sandcastle, avoiding disaster by mere inches. Murph continued his work unfazed, his long black hair in a ponytail to keep it out of his face as he worked. Unlike Seamus, his dark tan skin soaked up the sun. He'd brought an entire set of small sculpting tools to help with construction. And he'd strategically, put some distance from where a group of college kids had been playing volleyball all morning. The castle was nearly three feet tall, with five towers to fortify it. His tongue crept out of his mouth as he etched minor details onto the walls.

The sound of giggling brought Colt's attention to a young couple sunbathing together a few paces away. They couldn't seem to keep their hands off each other. The young woman giggling as the man tickled her with the biggest smile on his face. Their carefree feelings of joy felt like a distant memory.

Bringing his hands together above his head and shifting the position of his feet, Colt changed to warrior I pose. Everything was peaceful. Everything was so calm and *had been* so calm, but he couldn't shake the feeling that something was wrong. It was more than the caution from Jorah's words. It was like the world was off balance. Like the peace couldn't settle in him.

The volume of the old women talking to his left increased again, ruining any peace he was finding in his workout. They were both relaxing in lounge chairs with colorful drinks, gossiping away like no one else could hear them.

"Can you believe Bonnie didn't want us coming out here?" asked the old woman with a pink umbrella in her drink. The way she cackled sounded like she'd had a few too many of them.

The other old lady who was pouring out of her seat

replied, "She thought we'd get all kinds of trouble from that terror group down here. What were they called again . . . soul library, seal leopard?"

Sol Levante? Colt thought. *Their conversation just got more interesting.*

"No, no," replied the first woman. "They're called Sol Levante, and like I said, we don't have anything to worry about from them. Next, you're going to tell me we have to worry about the devils the locals are all so scared of." Both women burst out laughing.

It wasn't uncommon for people to blame the super-natural for things they didn't understand. But Colt hadn't experienced anything supernatural since they'd arrived.

The conversation quickly dissolved into more gossiping about their friends. Colt took a deep breath, changing to the tree pose, holding his hands high above his head and placing his left foot against his right thigh. Wobbling back and forth, Colt couldn't seem to keep his balance. There was still a pit in his stomach. He hated keeping things from his team, especially when he always expected them to be honest with him. Giving up on the tree pose, he spread his legs apart slightly and leaned forward, going into the downward dog.

Through his legs, he could see Grace, with her big movie-star sunglasses, lounging provocatively, with a harem of men attending to her every need. Her eyes never left her phone as she texted and posted selfies of herself. The Vigil chain she was wearing as an anklet shimmered in the light when she kicked her foot up. She changed how she wore it more than any Vigil Colt knew. Her harem did everything they could to get her attention away from the phone. It wasn't going to happen.

Standing up straight again, Colt took a deep breath through his nose, letting in the sweet scent in the air. *I need to relax.* Out of the corner of his eye, he caught something white moving.

His hands flew up, catching a volleyball before it hit him in the face. There were perks to keeping his guard up.

"Sorry about that," said a woman running over to get the ball. She was wearing a cute little yellow one-piece swimsuit. The only thing that set her apart from any of the other preppy college students he'd seen was the scar on the right side of her face that went from the corner of her mouth down the side of her chin.

"No problem." Colt handed the volleyball to her. She tucked a loose strand of her wavy blond hair behind her ear before taking the ball back.

The woman gave him a quick once over with her eyes. "Nice reflexes. We could use another player." She motioned to the other sand volleyball players. "Why don't you come and join us?"

Maybe I should *go play, get my mind off things.* His team too: they could use something to get them working together. Even now, they were close by, but still not doing anything together.

As he considered, several small brown and yellow birds darted out of the jungle, dragging a wave of fear behind them. The fear coming from the forest through his Animancer sense felt heavy, and it enveloped Colt. It was so sudden and overwhelming, not only from the animals, but from the trees and plants. "Sorry, maybe next time," he said to the woman. "I've got to get going." Colt's voice trailed off.

"Too bad." The girl playfully twirled a loose strand

of her hair. "I'm sure we'll get to play together another time."

Each step he took toward the jungle was heavier than the last. His survival instinct screamed for him to stop, and he paused at the edge of the jungle. He turned toward the stone path that led back to the city, the old brightly colored buildings. If he went to the hotel first, he could grab some equipment. Jorah didn't want them getting involved; he just needed to observe.

Even the sunlight didn't seem to want to enter; it was the middle of the day, but the darkness was almost tangible. It clung to every branch and leaf, making it almost impossible to identify anything more than a yard in.

Colt dug his feet into the sand, took a deep breath, and pressed forward into the darkness. The temperature dropped as the sunlight left his skin, replaced with goosebumps. He could not hear the crunch of the undergrowth beneath his feet. The birds and animals were gone or completely silent. Even the plants retreated deep inside of themselves, like they were hiding from the darkness.

Colt gently placed his hand against a tree trunk, listening for what it had to say. There was a tightness in the tree: it was pulling away from the outside world. Colt's own heartbeat started racing. A twig snapped in the distance. Releasing the tree and hunching down, Colt looked around for the source of the noise. Everything was still again.

Closing his eyes, Colt focused on Chi Chi: she was a house cat that he'd bonded with to gain her capability to see in the dark. The colors dulled as his eyes adjusted to the darkness, allowing him to see deeper and more clearly into the jungle. He looked up through the canopy of the trees. Maybe this was all aquatic naga setting a trap, or sinsimito waiting to strike. There weren't any blue scales or brown fur he could see, though, just more of the black shadows. Leaves rustled as something darted through the forest. It was fast enough that Colt couldn't see it, only the branches resting again where it had already been. A thick dark fog rolled in over the ground obscuring the forest floor.

Taking deep shallow breaths through his nose, Colt focused on letting his heartbeat faster: his muscles tightened and the smells of the forest became more distinct. Colt had practiced mastering the animal instinct technique for a couple of years now, allowing him to use and maintain the many skills he'd learned from animals all at once, for nearly an hour at a time. Each technique he'd learned from a different animal: sight in the dark from Chi Chi, enhanced hearing from an owl, increased speed and dexterity from a horse, and a superior smell from a coonhound named Rusty. His nose filled with the scent of decay and death. Gripping the tree, Colt scrambled up a tree to the canopy to get a better view of the bushes and understory.

In the distance, he could see a man standing next to a tree, wearing a fedora. Colt could feel the man watching him. His heart started racing. Edging toward the end of the branch, Colt planned his path through the trees to the man. Then several branches snapped behind him. Leaping into the air, he flipped around to face whomever, whatever, was behind him. Colt's muscles swelled, ready to strike as he landed on the ground. He kept his limbs close to his body, scrunched together, making himself a smaller target.

"Whoa there." Seamus tripped backward over some foliage.

Murph stood still, holding his hands in the air in a non-threatening gesture.

Grace delicately stepped over a fallen branch, using her phone's light to guide her. "What are you doing out here? It's gross."

For a moment, Colt felt relieved, letting out a sigh. "It's just you." Then he remembered what he'd seen, what had spooked him in the first place. Spinning around, he couldn't find the man in the fedora anywhere.

It *couldn't* be the same man. They were thousands of miles from Texas. It was probably a trick of the light.

"What is it?" asked Seamus, rushing up next to Colt. "What's out there?"

He's always a little too eager for a fight. "Nothing," said Colt. "I thought I saw something out here, but . . . Yeah, it's nothing. Why are all of you out here?"

"You just up and left the beach without telling us where you were going." Grace placed her hands on her hips.

"We were worried about you," Murph quietly added, his deep voice rumbling.

"It's really creepy here. Can we get going back to the nice, warm beach?" Grace rubbed her arms.

"Yeah, let's get out of here. I don't know about the rest of you, but I am hungry." Colt rubbed his stomach. He didn't want to keep his team from enjoying the trip any longer than necessary.

"Mm-hmm," replied Murph with a big smile as they started out of the forest.

"It *is* about lunchtime." Seamus sounded almost disappointed by that fact.

"I guess I could eat something." She continued to shuffle through the understory, avoiding everything she could.

Colt relaxed his muscles. He hadn't used animal instinct for long. But that didn't mean he was going to be any less sore. And he'd been in his head again. There was nothing to worry about out here. The other Vigil teams were right—Jorah was being overly cautious.

A low grumble and growl filled the silence of the jungle.

"You that hungry, Murph?" Colt chortled.

"That wasn't me."

All four of them stopped in their tracks. They slowly looked up. In the trees above them, were two glowing eyes looking down on them from the darkness of the canopy. Black slime dripped down, nearly reaching the ground before the strand broke from the source.

"Don't make any sudden moves." His Animancer sense told him the creature felt agitated, frustrated, and defensive. Colt slowly reached out to the tree next to him.

"What is it?" asked Seamus, puffing out his chest and stepping closer.

Grace grabbed the back of Seamus's arm, pulling him back. "Watch it Swab . . . *Seamus*. Don't escalate the situation." She clenched her hand tightly in a fist.

Reaching his hand toward the creature, Colt let out a few catlike growls. Carefully, he tore the bark off the tree he'd reached out to.

An orange and black spotted paw reached from the tree out into the light, claws extending and digging deep into the branch. The jaguar snarled, pulling its snout and face into the light; the black slime oozed, dripping out of its mouth. Its body movement was wrong. It clung tightly to the branch, struggling to maintain its balance.

"I think it's sick." Colt could feel something was off with the jaguar. It should have pounced on them before they even noticed it.

The jaguar hissed and snarled, sniffing the air in their direction. It crouched, finally preparing to pounce. Colt slapped the large piece of bark onto his forearm; Latching onto his arm, it grew thicker as it spread, until it encapsulated his entire forearm, creating a bracer that extended on top of his hand. Colt winced when the bark dug into his flesh, securing itself to him. The popping sound of the expanding bark settled as it folded over his knuckles.

Exploring the jungle in their beach clothes might not have been the best idea they'd had. Colt held his bark arm forward while waving his other hand behind him, signaling for the others to step back.

"What is coming out of that thing's mouth?" asked Grace. "Looks nasty."

The ears of the jaguar stopped twitching and its full attention turned to Grace.

"Murph, wall!" Colt cried out as the jaguar pounced.

The ground trembled and a wall of earth rose in front of Grace, Seamus, and Murph. The jaguar gracefully pushed off the wall with its paws, changing its trajectory toward Colt. Colt held strong, planting his feet firmly, using his bark arm as a shield. The jaguar hit, his jaw wrapping completely around his protected arm, Colt looked into the poor creature's eyes. It was in pain, suffering.

"I'm sorry," whispered Colt, then yelled, "Murph! Spike!"

The ground trembled again and a spike of stone emerged. Throwing his weight forward, Colt forced the jaguar into the spike. For a moment, the jaguar bit down harder and flailed its limbs, but soon the pressure against his arm loosened, the jaguar's movements slowing down until it was still. Gently, Colt lowered the body to the ground, letting it rest.

"What was wrong with that thing?" asked Seamus, stepping out from behind the wall. Water floated around his fists, and he held them up like he was starting a boxing match.

Murph kneeled next to the jaguar's head, dipping two of his fingers into the black sludge seeping out of the jaguar's mouth. He rubbed it between his fingers. "Dunno, but something is not right." He sniffed it and then pulled it away from his nose immediately. "It smells like it's been decaying for weeks."

"Do any of you have something we can collect that stuff with?" asked Colt.

Grace shrunk away from it with a look of disgust on her face, shaking her head. Seamus thought about it before shaking his head, too. Murph reached into his satchel, pulling out a bag of chips. Carefully opening the bag, he started pouring them into his mouth like a waterfall.

"Is this *really* the time for that?" asked Seamus.

The sound of Murph's crunching as he scarfed down the chips was all the answer he got.

"What, you want him to waste them?" asked Grace. Then she looked closer at the bag, exclaiming. "Nacho cheese?! Never mind—dump them. That's the worst flavor."

"That bag's not a bad idea." Colt tried not to laugh at Grace's outburst. He brushed the fur on the jaguar's head and closed its eyes.

Murph used his hand to scoop the black sludge into the bag and put it back in his satchel.

"After we get back to the hotel, I'll get that to the local

Vigil," said Colt, "and they can look into this. No need for us to ruin our vacation." Colt took a few steps back from the jaguar. "Grace."

She pulled a lighter out of her small purse, igniting it with a click. She coaxed the flame away from the lighter, levitating it above her palm, letting it grow. Then turning her open hand toward the body of the creature, a flame thrower erupted, devouring the corpse and the leaving nothing but ash and scorched earth once she was done.

COLT POUNDED HIS FIST ON THE RAILING OF HIS HOTEL-ROOM BALCONY
and spun on his heel to march back to his bed. The sun
was all but gone, setting on one more day. He wasn't any
closer to finding anything than he'd been when he started,
unless the black sludge in the chip bag turned out to be
something. It sat on the hotel dresser, taunting him; it
wasn't a "strange creature" like Jorah had asked him to
investigate, but there was something that wasn't right.
He couldn't think of anything like it and there were no
references to a substance that fit its description in the
Vigil records he'd searched. The local Vigil would arrive
any minute to pick it up. When he'd contacted them, they
told him they would send a couple of Vigil to pick up his
findings later that day. If it was anything, they'd send it up
the chain of command. But a sick animal wasn't enough
to worry Jorah about. Colt glanced down at his watch.
If the local Vigil weren't there soon, he'd need to go out
and get some coffee to wake himself up. The hotel bed
was much more enticing: he was still sore from using his
animal instincts.

He'd moved his search back to Sol Levante. His tablet
still displayed the local news reports he'd been reading,
anything he could find on them or strange creatures in the

area. From what he could see, Sol Levante was all talk and no bite. They looked like any other religious organization with lots of promises, but anytime he found mention of strange creatures, they simply dismissed it as a rumor. The more of these local blogs and vlogs he read and watched, it seemed like more and more people were joining their cause. The numbers of people disappearing in the area were growing as well. Sol Levante blamed the disappearances on the sins of the people and the government, saying that their sins brought demons down upon them. There were dozens of articles and blogs talking about the disappearances. Most of them were opinion articles, with little to no facts backing them up except for the missing person reports that were filed with the local police.

Connecting the disappearances and *demons* sounded more promising, likely just creatures that the locals didn't know how to explain. It seemed like Sol Levante was really just a bunch of ambulance chasers, calling the strange creatures demons to increase fear and using the fear to promote their own cause.

Grabbing his laptop, Colt pinned on a map all the places where *demons* had been sighted and any Sol Levante hot spots. That led him to nothing. There wasn't any pattern he could see—they just looked like random occurrences. The only thing he could see was that they seemed to occur in increasingly populated areas. Like they were gaining confidence.

Stretching and stepping away from his computer, Colt went back to the balcony, looking back over the cityscape. The city lights lit up the edges of the forest and the ocean, leaving large, empty black spots where the ocean and forest were dense. Normally, looking into the darkness didn't bother him at all, but there was something off here.

It was hard to tell at first, but as he looked closer, he saw there was a mist or a fog appearing in the forest. The same dark fog he saw before they found the sick jaguar. Just like before, a flock of birds flocked together, flying away from the jungle. A few moments later, he could see small woodland creatures flooding into the city streets, too.

The tourists filling the streets didn't seem to notice at all, laughing and drinking, having a good time; besides the vendors selling to them, there weren't any locals in the area. The fog was growing denser, blocking the light into the forest, already covering the ground near it. A steady hum of the world surrounded him from all the music and people talking, but he couldn't take his eyes off the fog. There was something sinister about it. The hair on the back of his neck stood up like a predator was nearby. The rush of thoughts and panic moving through Colt's mind muted the world. There were so many people, and they were all in danger. The fog continued to inch forward out of the trees, reaching toward the people.

Three loud thumps on the door made him jump and drop to the floor. He scrambled to his feet, finally felt awake and drew his knife, then moved as quietly as he could to peer out the peephole on the hotel door. Two men in brown jackets with their hoods up stood there. One of them kept checking the hall, looking from one end to the other. The second man was bouncing on the balls of his feet, keeping his eyes on the door.

Colt opened the door a crack. "Humanity's shield against the night."

"We are the Vigil." They held up their wrists, showing Colt their chains.

The darker tone of their skin confirmed that they were locals. The one closest to the door only had two additional chain links. One was white wood with purple swirls—lilac wood—and the second was a yellowish silver metal; ligantium. So, he was probably an Aeromancer. The other had a sterner and more serious look on his face beneath the hood. His chain had seven additional links; in the split second he showed it, the citrine crystal was the only link to stand out. *With that many links, could be a Shinigami.*

Opening the door, the rest of the way, Colt set his knife down.

"Qué más, Parce?" asked the first Vigil, walking through the door and grabbing Colt in a hug. "I'm Juan Carlos and this is Mateo."

"Colt." Struggling a bit, Colt finally broke free of Juan Carlos's hug. "Thank you for making your way out here. I know it's late."

"You found something strange," said Mateo in an authoritative tone. His English was much more refined than Juan Carlos's.

"Yeah, it's over here." Colt pointed to the chip bag, then picked it up and opened it, fiddling it around to allow the hotel's light into the bag. "We found this weird black substance in a sick jaguar's mouth. I couldn't find anything matching the description and smell in the databases."

"Chévere! That's awesome! What do you think it is? Something new, some sort of witches' magic ¿listo?" sputtered Juan Carlos, reaching into the bag.

"Juan Carlos." Mateo snapped. He waited until Juan Carlos pulled his hand away from the bag like it'd been slapped and then continued. "Thank you, Colt. We'll take things from here." Mateo took the chip bag from Colt, meticulously folding the top and closing it.

Another flock of birds fled the jungle, flying past the balcony. Colt could sense their fear. "You didn't notice anything strange when you came into town, did you?"

"No. Is there something more than your sick jaguar that you've seen?" asked Mateo.

"The fog outside doesn't seem natural to me," said Colt, walking back to the balcony.

Mateo and Juan Carlos followed him. "Parce!" Juan Carlos said. "This is a magnificent view! How'd you get it?" Juan Carlos's excitement and curiosity seemed to energize him.

Mateo studied the view, rubbing his chin. "Everything looks fine to me; you probably aren't used to the fog we have here, yet. We'll get this back to our facility and inspect it." Mateo held up the chip bag. "If you notice anything else strange, please notify us. Memento mori."

"Memento mori," replied Colt, standing straight.

Seeing that man in the fedora earlier was strange, but that could have easily been his mind playing tricks on him; he was *looking* for something to be off, just like the fog. Mateo turned and walked out the hotel-room door.

"How do you say, Rumbear . . . oh yes, go party, have fun, enjoy my country while you are here, Parce," Juan Carlos patted Colt on the shoulder as he followed Mateo out of the room.

Maybe I should *try harder to have some fun and enjoy my vacation.* Colt turned off his laptop and tablet. But *first, I am going to get some sleep.*

A high shriek of a scream shattered the calm of the night.

He ran to the balcony. *No . . . no, no, no.* He surveyed the area, looking for the source of the scream. Then there was another scream, this one followed by laughter. Three drunk college girls stumbled through the street below, doing their best to support each other. They screamed and laughed again. Colt let out a long, sheepish breath of relief.

Even this drunk trio works well together. I need to get some team exercises planned. It doesn't matter how new we are; we need to be ready.

Colt turned to get dressed for bed again, but the tree line caught his attention. The fog was still encroaching on the city streets; it was already taking over an outdoor café full of patrons. Leaning against a tree next to the café was the man in the fedora. He was there, no mistaking it. This couldn't be a coincidence; he was here; something was about to happen.

Colt pulled on his brown jacket, then took his knife and sheathed it at the back of his belt, using the jacket to conceal it. He opened the door to the hall just in time to see Grace leaving her room. The short pink dress and knee-high boots meant she was about to head out to a party.

"Grace, I need you to get the others and your gear and meet me at the café next to the jungle behind the hotel."

"Are you okay? You look like you've seen a ghost," she responded, looking up from her phone.

"Did you hear me?" asked Colt.

"Yeah, I heard you, but you don't look okay. I'll take the others and look around, but you should probably lie down."

"No. I need to catch the local Vigil before they get too far. I need to warn them. Just get Murph and Seamus. I'll meet you down there."

Mateo and Juan Carlos were nowhere to be seen in the

lobby or in front of the hotel. He'd have to go after the man in the fedora on his own. If he moved fast, he might catch him this time.

Running through the streets, Colt dodged and spun around people, pushing off the buildings to maintain his balance. He finally slowed down as he reached the café. Everyone around was carefree, eating together, having conversations. None of that mattered to Colt. If the man in the fedora had followed him from Texas, he was going to find him.

In the sea of heads, there wasn't a fedora in sight.

Above the sound of his heart beating in his ears, Colt heard a distinct clicking sound, like teeth snapping against each other. The snapping of teeth grew louder, cutting through the rest of the noise resonating around him. Farther off came more snapping; slowly, there was more and more, reverberating from the forest. Then there was the rustling of leaves from the thick fog. Colt's feet felt frozen to the ground. His mind begged his feet to move, but there was no response. It was a stronger wave of fear than even when he was in the jungle earlier that day. Silhouettes stretched up against the fog. Tall, elongated men. The stench of rot and death filled the air.

A pale hand with drawn out fingers reached out from the fog, twisting and curling toward the people. On the end of each finger was a long, curved hook like a talon. The muscles flexed under the thin, pale skin of its arms, clawing into the air as it pulled itself free as if from some unseen cage. A pale face emerged from the fog. Mouth gaping open, its jagged sharp teeth snapped, making the same loud clicking noises as it sharply clapped its jaw open and closed. There were two slits where a nose should have been, and two little dots looked out from its sunken in eyes. Colt could only stand there, watching. The creature was something out of a nightmare.

Lurching forward, it hunched down, keeping itself low as it came out of the fog. It sniffed deeply into the air before rearing its head back and letting out a blood-curdling scream. As the world fell silent, finally noticing the impending doom, the creature snapped its jaw together again three times.

Dread replaced the once jovial mood of the crowd as they stared at the creature slowly staggering toward them. Then a few of the tourists began screaming and running, giving way for the rest of the crowd to clamor over each other trying to escape.

Digging deep, Colt mustered his strength, channeling his abilities and the sturdy strength of an ox he'd met. He could feel the blood flowing through his muscles as they stretched and tightened.

He threw all his weight into a hit. His fist crashed into the creature's face with a loud cracking sound.

Pain shot through Colt's side: the creature's claws securely anchored into him. The pain from his side spread across his entire body as the creature tugged away at his flesh. Colt squirmed and twisted until he tore himself free of the creature.

Raising its blood-drenched claws up to its face, the creature's tongue ravenously licked at the blood. Then, filled with a new vigor, the creature screeched louder into the air with a more victorious ring.

Colt's strike against the creature had been strong enough that it should have snapped its neck, but the creature seemed all but unfazed by his attack. Colt grew tense. Whatever this was, it didn't feel like any creature he'd encountered before. All he could sense in the creature was hunger: no pain, no primal need for survival, just hunger. Colt took another swing, driving his fist into the gut of the creature. It snapped at him, opening its jaw wide, trying to catch any part of him. Hunger was still the only feeling emanating from the creature: even with two debilitating hits, still no pain, no concern. Scooting backward, Colt cradled his side. He kept pressure on the gashes, hoping that Grace and Murph would be there soon. More creatures were approaching. A flash of light drew his attention back toward the fleeing crowds.

Standing amid the crowd was Mateo, holding a large metal pole. It extended into a full staff with a full curved blade that unfolded and then ignited in flames. "¡Salgan de aquí! Everyone, get out of here!" He spun the scythe, getting ready to attack.

Dashing toward the first creature with the first swing, Mateo cut the creature's arm clean off. Then in a flashy display of spins, Mateo took off the creature's head with one clean slice.

The Shinigami were the elite of the Vigil. Mateo proved that with the ease he took in felling creature after creature. He went from one to the next, cutting them down. There was a sizzle as the flaming scythe went through them. Clenching his side, Colt took another step away, allowing Mateo the space he needed to evade the creature's gangly arms as they swiped at him. With each creature Mateo cut down, three more seemed to claw their way out of the jungle.

"Are you watching this guy too?" asked Grace as she, Murph, and Seamus ran up to him. "That's some serious pyromancy."

"I've never seen a Shinigami in action before." Seamus's entire focus was on Mateo. "Do they choose their own scythe, or do they have one assigned to them?"

Murph had put on a pair of brass knuckles and punched both of his fists into the ground. The stone from the road stretched up and covered over his forearms. Then he knocked his fists together, making a hollow thudding sound, and led with his left foot, ready to take some serious strikes. He lifted his fists in front of his face: they'd been getting better at the Piston Style, but this didn't seem like the time to be using it.

"Careful, Murph, they're more resilient than they look." Colt rubbed his hand, holding his side. "I hit one as hard as I could, and it didn't even slow it down."

Grace lifted Colt's hand, looking at his injury. "Keep pressure on that, and I'll tend to it once we're finished here." Her stance matched Murph's, raising her fists, drawing flames from the small fires left by Mateo. Letting the flames start at her knuckles and flow down her arms, she jabbed forward twice with her right fist, releasing big orange and yellow flares of fire.

Seamus started pulling the water from all the glasses and carafes. The water spindled from the different sources, gathering into his palm, freezing into a handle, extending a blade, creating a claymore of ice. "These things don't look too tough. Look how easily the Shinigami is offing them." He charged forward, hacking away at the nearest creature. It took him a few swings to cut it down.

Murph and Grace split up, attacking more of the creatures

exiting the jungle. There were so many of them. How could creatures with such hunger have remained hidden? The creatures didn't seem sapient, or even driven by instinct.

Watching the fight, their necks seemed to be their weak point, or maybe a powerful strike to the head. His team was finally making headway through the horde, nearing the edge of the jungle: Murph delivering devastating blows that caved in their skulls, Grace burning them beyond recognition, and Seamus breaking through the flesh he was freezing.

Colt's pride in their success was short-lived. They were pressing too fast, missing the creatures that were circling around them.

"Slow down! Don't let them get behind you!" called out Colt.

They're moving too fast, and they're too spread out. No one has anyone else's back. It's the desert naga all over again.

Gripping his side with one hand, Colt pulled out his knife with the other, taking it in a reverse grip. His team needed him, injury or no injury. He rushed, slamming his knife into the head of a creature that was flanking the group. It entered the creature's skull with a crunch, and he twisted the knife. There was a crack. The creature's body dropped to the ground. Black sludge dripped off Colt's blade. Bringing the blade to his nose, he confirmed it had the same rancid smell as the substance they took from the jaguar.

Colt almost fell as his collar was yanked backward, and he turned to see Mateo pulling him close. "You need to pull your team back; they are going to get killed out there!"

Then, holding his scythe high above his head, Mateo

ran ahead of Colt's team. In a fluid motion, he drove the blade into the ground. Five-foot flames erupted, creating a barrier in front of the creatures. The light of the flames flickered against their black beady eyes; they opened their mouths wide and screeched at the flames. Seamus took a position next to Mateo, and his ice claymore started sweating profusely against the barrier.

Mateo turned back to Colt. Colt couldn't hear what he was saying over the deafening screeches of the creatures, which grew louder with each passing moment. Colt knew he needed to step forward, ignore his injury, help his team or pull them back; but looking at his team, a memory of Nicky hit him so hard, he found his feet frozen to the ground again. Finally leaping through the flames, one creature dug its claws deep into Mateo's back. Mateo pushed Seamus out of the way as another creature leaped through the barrier, hooking itself into Mateo and holding his arm and scythe down. One after another swarmed Mateo, burying him in a pile of the creatures' bodies. Seamus scrambled backward, dropping his claymore. Grace held her hands out to support the barrier. Scooping Seamus up, Murph withdrew back to Colt. The stone coating over his hands and forearms cracked, falling apart.

Sweat was pouring off Grace's face, her arms were trembling. She couldn't hold out for much longer.

"Colt?" said Murph.

It was like a scene out of a nightmare, creatures charging at them cloaked in flame, clawing at them even as they dropped to the ground. There was no end to them spawning from the darkness.

A woman's voice cut through the chaos. "Fear not!" she said in English. "Though thy sins have born this blight, you can all be saved through the redeeming light of Sol Levante!" She was standing in a hotel balcony near the beach, draped in charcoal robes, looking down on the crowd and holding a staff with a glowing orange stone on the top. She tapped the staff on the ground twice and raised it into the air. A beam of light went from the top of the staff to the creatures. They screamed and shrilled but returned to the forest. The light followed them, driving them deeper into the trees. "All who believe and embrace the Creator's Light will be saved!"

Jorah mentioned that he thought Sol Levante had an artifact, but a mage of this caliber was something else. The pain in his side grew stronger, he could worry about that woman later.

Dropping to her knees, Grace let the flames die out. Seamus stepped away from Murph, standing up properly, pretentiously brushing the dirt off himself. They were in no condition to continue out here. "Murph," said Colt, "get Grace please, we're regrouping back at the hotel."

Murph gently approached and picked her up, carrying her back to the hotel. It was hard to tell that the body on the ground was Mateo's. If the creatures had their way, likely none of him would be left. This was going to be a hard one for the Vigil to cover up, but Colt's team needed to get out of the spotlight.

"That's right, run!" Seamus yelled into the jungle.

Colt groaned, pulling his hand away from his side. It was still wet and flowing. "Seamus, that means you, too. Back to the hotel."

Even from just outside the hotel, they could faintly hear the member of Sol Levante continuing her recruitment speech. It drew people to her, leaving the hotel in droves. Down the street, others opened windows so they could hear her. Having everyone so preoccupied with Sol Levante, they could get back to their floor with almost no one seeing them.

"You can put me down." Grace said just outside their rooms, wobbling a bit. She looked like she did when she was drunk. "Colt, let me look at you."

Peeling back the strips of cloth to look at the wound, Grace's face changed to a grimace. Colt held his jacket back, giving her more space to work. "At least that thing didn't rip apart my jacket. This is one of my favorites."

"Really," snapped Grace.

"Sorry." Colt put on a cheesy smile. "If you could just fix me up quick—I don't think this is over yet."

"This is bad, Colt, like, terrible. I'll do what I can, but we should really get you to a hospital. Sit down."

He sat on the floor, leaning back against the wall. Warmth spread across Colt's side as Grace used her pyromancy to start the healing process. "Thanks." It was soothing. The warmth continued through his body, comforting his pains.

Murph stood vigilant in the hall with his arms crossed—a stoic guardian, there to protect. He cleared his throat.

"You've *got* to be kidding me." Grace sounded even more annoyed than usual.

Colt looked up. At the end of the hall, two people approached in cloaks like the Sol Levante speaker, only black instead of charcoal. They seemed to glide as they walked toward them. When they got closer, the uneasy feeling returned, it was the same he kept feeling. The man in the fedora, the fog, the creatures, something was very wrong.

One of the cloaked men was shorter and the other tall and slender; he had to be at least six and a half feet tall.

His eerie voice filled the hall. "All who believe and embrace the Creator's Light will be saved!"

Murph moved between the people, Colt guessed they were Sol Levante acolytes, and his team. He cracked his knuckles, sizing them up.

"They're here to help, Murph," called out Seamus. "I brought them here."

Colt looked at Seamus in surprise, but he didn't have the energy to fight against the strangers help.

"Brother, please," said the woman from the balcony, stepping out from behind the two acolytes. "We don't mean you any harm. I saw what you did to protect the people of this city." She turned to Seamus and smiled. "All of you were so gallant and skilled in your defense against the demons. I wanted to see if we could assist you."

Murph looked back at Colt and Grace, raising his eyebrows and tilting his head in question.

Colt sighed. Blood was still flowing from his side; Grace pressed her hands tighter against him. "He won't go to a hospital, and I don't know that there is much more that I can do for him."

Despite Colt's reservations about letting Sol Levante help, he felt weak. If there was anything they could do, this was the time. He nodded to Murph. Murph lumbered to the side, letting the woman through.

"Thank the Creator we got here when we did. May I?" She motioned for Grace to move aside.

Grace locked eyes with Colt. "Go ahead," he said weakly.

"Don't worry, brother: through the Creator, all things are possible." She brushed aside her black hair from her face so she could examine him. The stone on top of her staff glowed orange again. She placed her hand on it, closed her eyes, and whispered. "Creators Light, make this man who has defended against the destroyers whole." Her eyes opened, irises changing from a chocolate color to glowing the same as the stone. The stone's glow moved from the stone to her hand, and she lifted it away. She pressed it against Colt's side.

A feeling of ecstasy raced through Colts' body, all his pain and worries melted away, replaced by a jubilant warmth. He gasped, and even the air tasted sweeter as it passed through his mouth. The world darkened around him. As he passed out, the woman spoke again.

"Praise be to the Creator!"

"Praise be!" echoed the acolytes.

THE CITRUSY, SALTY SCENT OF THE OCEAN BREEZE TICKLED COLT'S nose as he woke up. He could hear the soft crashing of the waves against the beach. He wasn't sure if it was because of how tired he was, but the hotel bed was softer than he remembered.

The moment he opened his eyes, he knew he wasn't in his hotel room. The ceiling was a bright white, with large, dark tiles composing the wall to the right and behind him. Ahead of him and to his left were glass panels that went from floor to ceiling, revealing a glorious view overlooking the ocean. One panel was open, allowing the breeze to enter the room.

"We brought you to our compound to make sure that your recovery went smoothly. I hope you don't mind." He hadn't noticed the woman who had healed him sitting in a chair near the door. She was wearing the same charcoal robes as when he first saw her but didn't have any shoes on.

"No, no." He lifted his shirt to look at where the creature had attacked him. It was completely healed. There wasn't even a scar. "That's amazing, thank you."

"Don't thank me, thank the Creator. It was his will that you be healed."

"If I see him, I certainly will." Colt cleared his throat.

"With everything going on, I don't think I ever got your name."

She smiled, standing up, clearing her black hair from her face. "Orator Meg. Your friends told me that your name is Colt."

"Nice to meet you, Orator Meg." Colt pulled the sheets off. They'd dressed him in a white gi.

"We cleaned your clothes as best we could. They're in the closet. We weren't able to save your shirt. There was a big gash in the side. You and your friends did rather well against the demons."

Colt chuckled. *Demons! I don't know what monsters those were, but they weren't demons.* "Thank you. We've had some experience."

"Vigil have plenty of experience with the creatures of this world, but those weren't of this world. It takes more than the training they give you to be successful against the demons. Vampires, werewolves, even pixies have a sense of self preservation. Demons only care to satisfy their needs."

"You seem to have a solid understanding of the Vigil." Colt looked around outside the window. He didn't recognize any of the landscape. "Where are we exactly?"

"This is our sanctuary. A place where we can train and learn in safety from the world and the darkness. And yes, your companions are here. It took us almost a whole day to convince the big one . . . Murph—that he could go get some sleep and that you would be safe in our care. We'll be meeting them soon enough. When I saw you waking, I had some of our disciples go fetch them."

"No, let them sleep. They've had a long night," he said, springing from the bed. This was the best Colt had felt in years. It was like when he was using his animal instincts. His body seemed to move before he even finished the thought. Suddenly, his head felt light. He used the bed to steady himself.

"We should get you some fresh air." She motioned to the balcony and then led him out to view the property.

The compound sat on the side of a mountain overlooking the coast, and a large stone structure sat on a small island connected to the mainland, with a cliff on one side. The structure was like ancient Aztec or Mayan temple. There was a large stone path with stairs that led along the coast and up to the base of the structure.

"Beautiful, isn't it? One of the ancient Temples of Sol. A monument to the Creator, we built this sanctuary here so we could be close to it. I can take you there later if you'd like. It's a special place."

"Is that where you got the staff, the one that allowed you to heal me?" *With something like that, I can help her: get her out of the hospital.* He ran his hand down his side again. This was stronger healing magic than he'd ever come across.

"You have it all wrong. The staff was merely a tool for us to receive the Creator's Light."

"So, you don't know where the staff is from?"

Orator Meg tucked a stray strand of hair behind her ear. "You must be hungry; the healing process can take a lot out of the recipient, too. Come along, then."

"Do I have a choice?" Hidden among the trees stood armed guards and security fences. If this was the security he could see, there would be plenty of others they were hiding. Colt took one last look over the property before he followed Orator Meg back into the room.

"You aren't prisoners, if that's what you're asking. Think of yourselves as our guests who can leave whenever they'd like. This room is yours to use for as long as you need. Your phone and the other items we found you with are all in the closet. If you can get service, please make any calls you'd like." She pointed to the closet.

Colt opened the closet; his jacket, his pants, shoes—they were all there.

She turned away from him to face the door. "You may change into your clothes if you'd like. Then I would appreciate it if you'd join me for our evening meal."

Colt felt through the jacket; his phone was in one pocket. Sure enough, there wasn't any signal. "Thank you. I'll join you for a meal. I'll change first, though." Keeping the top half of the gi, Colt changed back into his pants, shoes, and jacket.

"For the security of the sanctuary, we won't be returning your weapons until you leave. I hope you understand. If you decide to walk outside the sanctuary, please make sure you bring one of our security personnel with you. We are safe within the walls, but we've seen demons near the grounds."

"Demons here?" Colt fixed and straightened his jacket.

"Where there is greater light, there is also greater shadow until the light can overcome it completely."

Is everything she says so dramatic? There wasn't anything in the closet or room that looked like it could be used as a weapon, let alone be concealed. "Alright, I'm ready to go."

"Excellent." She opened the door to the long hall. Opposite his door were large glass panes that went from floor to ceiling like those in his room, separating him from a large grassy courtyard filled with a few benches and stone statues along the perimeter.

Two acolytes in black robes were waiting outside the door for them. They followed as Colt followed Orator Meg.

They passed several more doors that looked identical to his own as Orator Meg led him deeper into the sanctuary. Murals and paintings were between each of the doors in the hall. They all appeared to be representations of different historical magical events. Some Colt recognized as some of the great hunts and purges of the past, others didn't seem to represent anything he knew.

"These paintings and other artifacts also find safety here in our sanctuary, lest we lose the history and prophecies they hold." She let her hand brush against the golden frame of one picture.

Another mural caught his attention over the others. He stopped, taking a closer look. Despite the cult vibe Meg and the sanctuary gave, these paintings looked like the genuine article.

Orator Meg hovered behind him. "That is one of my favorites."

"It is beautiful," he said, entranced by the work. It had the Temple of Sol on the island in the background, with seven people standing in front of it, light beaming from each of them. Below them were the symbols for each of the six mage elements: Fire, Water, Earth, Air, Life, and Energy. Below the seventh person in the middle was the symbol of the Orasen. It looked like a lightning bolt with extra branches connected to the center.

"The seven warriors of light," said Mateo, walking up behind him as the acolytes parted. He wore the same white gi that Colt wore when he woke up.

Colt jumped, taking a step to the side. "I thought you were dead."

He held up his chain bracelet as evidence "No, still alive. Sol Levante takes care of its own."

Meg flung her arms around Mateo, giving him a hug. "I'm so glad you're recovering well."

Mateo took a step back from Meg. "Thanks to you, my lady." He put his pointer and middle finger against the bridge of his nose, bowing his head.

Colt watched Mateo curiously. Everything looked peaceful and in order, but in his gut, something felt wrong.

"Sol Levante is more akin to the Vigil than any care to admit," said Mateo. "We slay monsters, they hunt demons, we're all trying to protect humanity, so why not work together? Together: like the seven warriors of light who banished the demonic hordes from this world."

"Well said; I don't think I could have said it better." Orator Meg paused as an acolyte whispered something in her ear. "I need to take care of a few things before our evening meal. Mateo, please escort Colt to the main conference room?"

"Of course."

"This shouldn't take long. I'll meet you there. Mateo will be a great guide for you." Orator Meg gave Mateo the same Sol Levante salute he had given her and left with her guard.

"This is the symbol of the Orasen." Colt pointed at the symbol below the central figure in the middle of the mural. "That would make these the Seraphim, not the *seven warriors of light*. All the myths about them are just that: myths, stories to give people hope from the past."

"Plenty of Vigil believe the myths. Is it so hard to believe that some of the myths about them are true?"

Colt grunted. "Are all the Vigil in this area a part of Sol Levante?"

"Spend some time here. Get to know them before passing your last judgment. It might surprise you what you find. But don't wander off too far while you're here. I might not be there to save you next time." Colt huffed, still studying the mural. "Oh, and the grass feels much nicer in your bare feet."

Colt looked down; Mateo was barefoot, just like Orator Meg. Everything was clean and calm here, but Colt couldn't ignore his training, his instincts, and something still didn't feel right. It was the same feeling he had whenever the "demons" were near, but he knew they couldn't be here. At least not inside.

"Step to it." Mateo gently smacked Colt in the back. "We can't sit around looking at paintings all day."

Colt chuckled, following him.

As Mateo led Colt farther into the sanctuary, he pointed out common areas and classrooms full of people dressed in the same white gi's with no shoes on; they walked quietly through the halls, greeting each other warmly, while his sneakers made the occasional squeaking noise whenever they moved to a hard floor.

Some classes looked like they were learning about herbs and potions. There was another class that was doing yoga, another researching crystals. Each of them giving praise to the Creator and declaring their devotion. Each class they passed had at least one acolyte invite him to join, in the friendliest manner. He politely declined each one and continued on his way.

If he had to be here, he might as well look around and

try to get more information about the staff. It could be the artifact Jorah was looking into. And despite his reservations, one thought rose out and would not be quieted: It could be a cure for Nicki.

He should have been in that hospital bed, not her.

That staff left him without a scar and basically brought Mateo back to life. And it might not be the only artifact they had if they were letting Orator Meg bring it with her away from the sanctuary. Though none of the classes seemed to do any learning or training with artifacts.

One class finally caught Colt's attention. At first, he thought it was another group doing yoga. But this was something different. This was combat training on a large scale, with at least fifty people in the room. Juan Carlos was at the front, teaching them Vigil techniques.

"He really enjoys teaching that class. Wait here a moment." Mateo entered the room and headed toward Juan Carlos.

"Preparing to face the darkness is just as important as finding balance with oneself and devotion to the Creator," said a male disciple with messy brown hair, stepping up to Colt.

"That's understandable." Colt's eyes darted around for any excuse he could use to walk away from this conversation.

"If you'd just worn the gi, not as many people would keep coming up and talking to you."

That might have been the most honest statement Colt had heard all day. "I just feel more comfortable in my own clothes."

The disciple looked him over. "Just not your shirt."

Chuckling, he replied, "I'm Colt."

"Vaughn." He shook Colt's hand.

"You don't quite sound like the other believers." Colt lowered the volume of his voice, checking to make sure no one was too close.

"We all show our belief in our own ways." Vaughn took hold of the front of Colt's gi before turning him. So they were facing each other. "Let me help you fix that; they can be tricky." Vaughn's gray eyes looked over both of Colt's shoulders before he whispered, "Be careful who you trust. *Trust*. Right now, trust is the most important thing."

"Are you, did Jor . . "

"Your companion's coming back." Vaughn ran his hand through his messy brown hair, then scratched the stubble on his chin. "Look, I should really get back to my superiors before it gets too late."

"Thank you for the help. Sometimes it's hard to see what is right in front of you. How was I wearing this incorrectly?"

"Well, it sometimes takes just one person to call something to our attention when so many others have looked the other way."

He took a step back and bowed at Colt. Then he jogged down the hall, disappearing into a sea of disciples.

Mateo suddenly surprised Colt, motioning down the hall with both his hands. "We're close to the main conference room, and we don't want to get caught in the dinner rush."

Colt was almost running to keep up with Mateo as they went down another hall. Almost on cue, a herd of disciples rounded the corner, filling the entire hall behind him. This didn't make his search about the staff any easier. They whispered to each other, looking at him as they walked by, giving him a wide berth as they passed.

"Colt!" shouted Grace. He turned, looking for her, but

couldn't seem to find her in the crowd. There were so many people in the gi's from all different backgrounds and races. She just blended in. "Colt!" Her hand shot into the air. She waved at him from across the waves of disciples. He ran to her, leaving Mateo behind in the crowd. She gave him a big hug, clutching him. "We have to get out of here, Colt."

Letting go of her, he replied, "I don't know. I think you pull off the gi rather well."

"Of course I do, but have you tried to use your phone? There's no service, Colt . . . No service, no Wi-Fi? It's barbaric and inhumane. No one should be forced to live like this." She waved her phone in Colt's face, pleading her case.

"That sounds *awful*."

"Don't you patronize me. If it wasn't for me, you wouldn't have held out last night long enough for them to use that stick on you."

"Sorry, Grace. Do you know where Murph or Seamus are? I haven't seen them yet."

"I thought Murph was with you. He was the last time I saw him. Hey, how'd you get your clothes back?"

Colt straightened out his jacket, pulling it forward while playfully puffing out his chest. "They were in my closet. Where are yours?"

"They took them for cleaning and haven't brought them back yet. I told them my dress was dry-clean only, and the boots are real leather. The jacket, well, it's standard issue, so it doesn't really matter."

"I wouldn't stay too attached to that dress."

"It is my favorite pink dress . . " Grace trailed off, then started inhaling and exhaling deeply. "It's fine, not like our vacation is being ruined or anything." Colt sucked in through his teeth. Then the color began draining from his face as he realized what his reaction to her word *vacation* had done. "We *are* out here on a vacation, aren't we, *Colt*?"

"Is that Murph over there?" he asked, looking down the hall. Not only was Murph towering over the rest of the crowd, but he was back in his own clothes: maroon jeans, brown jacket, and his work boots.

"He's got *his* things. Where are mine?"

"I'm sure they'll get them back to you soon." Colt watched the never-ending stream of disciples flowing past them. "Where are these people going? Where did they come from?"

Mateo had finally fought his way through the crowd to Colt's side. "This is the fastest way to the dining hall. They're all coming from their classes, meditation time, whatever they were doing. This place only serves meals at certain times, and if you miss it, you're out of luck." Mateo's voice sounded like he spoke from experience, his eyes following the crowds toward the cafeteria.

That explained why Murph hadn't noticed them yet. He was most likely lost in his imagination about what the cooks had prepared.

Colt needed time to debrief with his team, *away* from Mateo. "You said we're close. If you point us in the right direction, we can find our way to the conference room. You should probably get going so you don't miss dinner."

"Gracias, Colt. It is the last door on the left at the end of this hall." Then Mateo pointed past Murph. "You should collect him before he rushes off to the cafeteria."

"We'll grab him when he comes by." Colt waited until Mateo was gone to ask Grace. "Have you seen Seamus?"

"He's been all over the place, really taking it all in. Especially with that Orator girl." She rolled her eyes.

"Does our boy have a little crush?"

"More like an infatuation with power." She took a step closer to Colt, avoiding a disciple. "Something is off here," she whispered.

"What, not enough people on their phones?" Colt already knew the feeling she was talking about, but he joked, trying to put her at ease. She raised her eyebrow at him. "Okay," he said seriously, "we're getting out of here."

The flood of disciples parted as five acolytes in black robes marched down the center of the hall. Each of them was carrying a silver serving dish covered with a cloche. They approached Colt and Grace and the leader of the group extended his pointer and middle finger, placing them between his eyebrows, and bowed his head. "Senior Colt, we are ready for you and your companions, if you will follow us."

"That smells delicious." Murph showed up and leaned over Colt's head, sniffing. "What is that? Smells fried and delicious: ah, empanadas. Yes."

Food brought Murph faster than anything else Colt knew.

"We just need our other companion, Seamus." Colt looked around for him.

"He'll be along shortly," said the acolyte, and he led them into a room with a large conference table. At the head of the table was Orator Meg.

"I'm so pleased that you could join me." She motioned for them to take a seat.

Murph and Grace waited until Colt took a seat before sitting across from and next to him. The acolytes set the trays down in front of them, lifting the lids to reveal the empanadas with Spanish rice, black beans, and creamy coleslaw with a side of chimichurri sauce.

"I knew it." Murph's shoulders bounced blissfully.

Colt scanned the room. It looked simple and clean, just like the rest of the sanctuary. There were two doors that led into the room, both leading out into the main hallway. The back of the room was a solid wall, and on either side were large floor-to-ceiling windows. They would be the best option for escape if needed. The plates of food brought more color and life than anything else he'd seen here. He realized now that the colors on the paintings and murals had seemed muted. A pit of anxiety formed in his stomach, with the acolytes in black robes still looming over them, and still no sign of Seamus.

"No need to wait for Seamus, he'll be along soon," Orator Meg said as though she was reading Colt's thoughts.

Murphy's eyes opened wide, begging Colt for permission to eat.

Orator Meg took a bite of her meal. "I've never understood people's hesitation. If we wanted to do you harm, there were plenty of opportunities before now."

So, the fact that they hadn't tried to kill them yet meant that they either wanted something from them first or they were true to their word.

With a gentle nod, Colt gave Murph permission. He shoveled food into his mouth while Colt and Grace continued to patiently wait.

"Please excuse me for any brashness earlier. I didn't recognize the talent that was before me. Colton Leigh, Grace Jones, Enzo Murphy, and Seamus Hayes. That's a lot of Vigil royalty for one team."

"I guess there's enough service out here for you to do some homework on us." Grace crossed her arms. "But you're going to have to do better than that to impress us."

Meg picked up her napkin, gently dabbing her face. "I meant no offense. We try to do our best with the limited resources we have here. What we could do with a *working* phone."

Colt tensed as Meg raised her hand in the air, signaling one of the acolytes. He opened the door, letting in a disciple carefully carrying Grace's pink dress, brown boots, and brown jacket.

"Thank you." Colt let himself relax. He stared at Grace until her eyes finally met his, giving her a silent order to back down. She shrunk down in her seat submissively.

The disciples set the bundle of Grace's clothes down next to her. Colt cleared his throat.

"Thanks," she muttered.

"Grace, my dear, you may always speak your mind here. Colt, you don't need to control, or be so controlling over your team. I promise they are safe. You all are our guests here."

On cue, another door opened, letting Seamus in. Unlike the other gi's, his was a light blue with dark-navy trim. He was beaming with excitement.

"Orator Meg, please excuse my tardiness." He bowed his head, putting his pointer and middle fingers on the bridge of his nose, performing the same Sol Levante salute. "I was so taken in with the magnificence of this place, I lost track of time."

"No need to apologize. We were just getting started. Have a seat and enjoy your meal. This place truly was set aside by the Creator for us." Orator Meg closed her eyes, lifting her hands up while tilting her head back. "Praise be to the Creator and the light we've been gifted with."

Seamus took the open chair next to Murph, scooting it a few inches away from him.

"You've been extremely hospitable." Colt looked uneasily down at his untouched plate. "But I think it's about time we get on our way."

Orator Meg lowered her hands and rested her gaze on Colt with a wide smile. "Like I mentioned, you are guests here. You may leave whenever you like." Something was unsettling about Meg's smile. It wasn't her lips, or the smile itself, but the coldness in her eyes. "However, I'd recommend you wait until the morning when our trucks can bring you into town while they pick up supplies."

"I think we can manage." Colt motioned to his team with his head that it was time to leave.

Murph started to stand, packing his cheeks with food like a chipmunk. Seamus looked embarrassed. He stayed sitting, shielding his face from Murph with his hand.

"Don't worry, Colt," said Orator Meg. "She isn't going anywhere. She'll still be waiting for you, even if you stay here for one night."

Colt froze in the act of rising to leave, the blood draining from hiss face.

Grace stopped folding her napkin around an empanada. "We're done here."

Orator Meg turned to Grace. "Aren't you tired of living in your sister's shadow?"

"Sorry?"

"Kat Jones, the Claw of the Vigil," clarified Meg. "It must be hard having your younger sister overshadow you."

The blood rushed to Grace's face, turning it a deep scarlet color. The surrounding temperature rose. Colt locked eyes with her and shook his head.

Orator Meg waited until Grace's face turned back to a pinker shade before continuing. "I mean no offense. The world can be an unfair place. We seek to help this imbalance."

"And how would some *cult* fix that?" snapped Grace. Heat still radiated off her.

Murph stopped chewing, his cheeks packed with food. The tension in the room rose with the temperature; the scarlet color returned to Grace's face.

The acolytes in the room easily outnumbered them, and each one stood ready to intervene should anything happen. Colt's muscles tensed and his focus tightened, expecting a fight. "*Grace!*"

"It's alright Colt, she is free to speak her mind here, as are all of you." Meg exchanged a quick glance with the acolytes in the room. Each of them took a step back from the table. "The truth can be difficult to hear, but once we accept it, truth grants us such sweet freedom. Many feel that religion oppresses. I can promise you that the Creator brings release and restitution. It has for these people of Colombia, and it can for your people too, Murph."

Nervously, Murph gulped down the food in his mouth. "What?" A few crumbs tumbled out of his mouth.

"It wasn't enough that your people's land was colonized. Then they placed them on reservations, showing their 'mercy.' It was nothing more than insult to injury. Your family, your sister, could have better. She could get a proper education rather than feeling caged on the reservation." Meg took a moment to take a bite of her food.

How do they know so much about us? Bringing up Grace's sister, Kat, was easy to guess, but knowing about Nicki and Murph's family? They weren't in the Vigil public records.

"We could help each one of you. Seamus, with us, you'll get the respect you deserve. Murph, together we can get your people restitution and a new future. Grace, *your* name could be known around the world. And for you, Colt, we can give Nicole—sorry, Nicki the cure the Vigil can't."

Despite himself, Colt found himself actually considering her offer. Treating the gash on his side without even leaving a scar, bringing Mateo back from the brink of death: Sol Levante had proven their prowess in the healing arts. *Could they help Nicki?*

Orator Meg snapped her fingers. The acolytes stepped forward, placing tablets in front of Grace, Murph, and Seamus. Eagerly Seamus started scrolling through his, excitement showing more and more on his face. Murph took a more cautious approach, reading what was on the screen carefully. Grace left hers sitting on the table. There were charts and graphs of projections on it.

"If you swipe to the next page, Murph, you'll see that we've prepared a full ride scholarship for Tiva to any school of her choosing. The reports on the first screen are our assessments and recommendations on how to change the laws to get your people their restitution." Murph swiped to the next page and dug deeply into the information, ignoring everything else. Orator Meg turned to Grace. "Grace, we've outlined a strategy that we believe will increase your followers by several million by the end of the year. These are early projections, but we are confident that we can reach them."

Looking at his team Colt felt even more conflicted than before. *Are they really here to help?*

"I know that this seems too good to be true, and I'm sure you're wondering what the cost for this is." The way Orator Meg spoke was as though she could read his thoughts. "We ask for nothing more than what you were already willing to give. Your loyalty and willingness to stand with us against the demons that seek to plague humanity. If you help us, we are more than pleased to use our resources to help you."

"Okay, okay." Colt hesitated, trying to collect his thoughts. "What specifically would you need from us?"

"We'll need all of you to formally swear your allegiance to the Creator. After that, you'll need to answer the call whenever you're summoned to assist. We can have the ceremony for the rest of you tomorrow, but we have a special ceremony planned for Seamus this evening."

"*Special* ceremony?" questioned Grace.

Orator Meg gave her a confused look. "Of course, we'll honor him with a special ceremony. He is a descendant of a warrior of light."

"*Him?*" asked Grace Seamus beamed with pride at Orator Meg's statement. "After tonight, people will understand, and I will help bring Sol Levante to the world."

"The Creator has brought such a fortune to us with your arrival," said Orator Meg. "The Creator's Light and understanding are far greater than our own. I'd love to have you all join this evening, but first you'd need to swear fealty as Seamus already has." Orator Meg radiated joy while she spoke. She was on top of the world.

This was all happening so fast. Colt just needed to think. Orator Meg continued to spout details of what was happening and the dogma of Sol Levante, but Colt's mind was elsewhere. Nothing about Sol Levante seemed wrong on the surface: they wanted to help him, his team . . . Nicki. They'd proven that they had the resources to do it all. But after everything they'd shown him, something still felt wrong. He tried to reconcile this feeling with logic.

It didn't add up in his head. Was he being swayed by his hope for Nicki?

An acolyte interrupted Orator Meg, whispering something in her ear. Her face soured. "I don't expect any of you to decide this evening. The sanctuary and all her facilities are open to you. If you'll excuse me, I have some urgent matters to attend to."

Acolytes summoned Seamus away to prepare for the evening's ceremony once Orator Meg left the room. The three of them sat, lost in their own thoughts, sitting silently for almost half an hour, when Grace finally asked, "So what are we going to do?"

"What do you guys think?" asked Colt, leaning back in his seat. He was tired of thinking around in circles.

Grace balled both of her hands into fists. "They're too happy. They're up to something. And that Meg, she's so smug. Just listen to how she talks."

"They clearly have resources, and the capability to affect change." Murph paused, leaning forward with his head down. "I believe they can make all of our dreams come to fruition."

They were both right. Colt had hoped they would've provided more insight than he already had. Instead, Grace and Murph echoed his own conflicting thoughts.

Murph sat up. "Mateo joined them, and he's Vigil too: a powerful pyromancer and Shinigami."

"Shinigami aren't as infallible as you think." Grace's voice had an icy edge. "They can be just as greedy and self-interested as anyone else."

Colt's thoughts finally settled. "She keeps telling us exactly what we want to hear." Colt cut in. "Sol Levante is offering us everything we want, and what is the cost? Our fealty, our blind obedience." He shook his head, coming to a decision. "I think it's time for us to leave."

Colt stood up and walked to the door, where two acolytes were standing. "Please have our things brought to us. We are ready to leave now."

The acolytes stepped closer together, blocking him from the door. "Orator Meg has requested that you stay in this room until they complete the ceremony."

Despite Murph's obvious objections, he was loyal to a fault. Grace and Murph both stood up, ready to follow, to fight, no hesitation. The other three acolytes in the room stood at attention and drew out daggers.

"We're on the third floor," said one of the acolytes, smirking. "No ground for you to grab here, Terramancer. No flames for you either, Pyromancer. So, what do you expect to do?"

"What they were trained to do." Colt smiled smugly.

Murph turned, grabbing two of the acolytes by their robes, lifting them into the air before smashing them against the ground. Grace grabbed the other acolyte by the wrist, turning their dagger back on them, into their chest.

Colt didn't look back at them, instead keeping his focus on the two acolytes at the door. Panic set in on their faces, and one of them opened the door. "We need reinforce-men . . "

His sentence cut short as Vaughn drove a disc blade into his chest. Then he shoved his second disc blade into the other acolyte before entering the room.

"Come on then," Vaughn said. "We've got work to do."

"Sorry, who are you?" asked Grace, pulling her dagger out and cleaning it with the acolyte's robes.

"That's Magamalirel." Murph said, pointing at the disc blades. They were both connected by chains that came together on a ring which Vaughn wore on his right arm. "He's a Seraph."

"I'm Vaughn, one of the Seraph, yes. And you're Grace, he's Colt, and he's Murph. Now that we're all acquainted, can we get going before Meg does something especially stupid?"

"We need our things," said Colt.

"Luckily for you, I swung by the armory on my way here." Vaughn pulled a large duffle bag into the room. "All of your things are there, including your clothes."

"Thank you." Murph opened the bag, pulling out his axe and jacket. He tossed Colt his sword.

Grace pulled the bag away from Murph delicately, pulling out her pink dress and her boots. "Yeah thanks."

"How long until reinforcements show up?" asked Vaughn, watching the door.

Grace and Murph turned around, changing their clothes as Colt strapped on his sword. "What reinforcements?"

"I told you to contact your superiors. I don't know how I could have made it any more obvious."

"*Obvious*? You *never* told me that." Colt shook his head. "Can you tell us what is going on here?"

"Meg is trying to make a power play against Lux Dei Isom." Colt gave him a confused look. "Lux Dei Isom: the leader of Sol Levante. Did you do any sort of research before coming out here?"

In all the research Colt had done, he'd never thought to look into who was in charge of Sol Levante. In hindsight, it should have been an obvious move. "What kind of power play?"

"The kind where she thinks that by using Seamus's blood, she'll be able to control the creatures they pull through the portals. We need to get to the temple and stop her from sacrificing Seamus before it's too late."

"Why should we trust you?" asked Grace, putting on her brown hoodie.

"Saving your lives wasn't good enough?"

"*They* saved our lives, too," said Murph, pointing at the dead acolytes.

"You may have a point there," replied Vaughn.

"If you're finished, we need a plan." Colt gave a stern look to both Grace and Murph.

"I thought reinforcements were on the way, or I wouldn't have made such a scene. I still don't know how she's summoning the creatures, but I know that tonight's ritual requires Seamus. If we stop her from getting his blood, we can stop them, for now."

Sol Levante is the one summoning those creatures? Colt put a pin in that information for later. He tried to remember everything he'd seen in the sanctuary. "There's got to be a way to get a message out. Do any of you know how they contact the outside world?"

The pressure in the room suddenly changed. "Get down!" Vaughn stretched his hands forward, knocking them all down with a gust of wind.

Three arrows flew into the room through the open door, sticking deep into the walls. They all had black and red feathers. Aeromancers could use their abilities to turn arrows around corners, so they couldn't see their attacker.

Vaughn used his abilities to throw his voice out into the hall. "You're getting better Jamie, you hit a wall that time." Two more arrows flew into the room, digging deep into the wall as they hit.

"I wasn't expecting you here, Vaughn." Jamie's voice sounded like she was in the room. It sounded familiar to Colt, somehow. "Meg's been drawing so much attention lately I was thinking she'd bring us the Shadow. But you and a few little Vigil will be good enough."

Colt had heard of Shadow sightings from all over the world. The Shadow had left dozens of dead Vigil and Hidden in his wake, but there were other sightings no one understood. His movements had no rhyme or reason.

Another arrow flew through the room.

Vaughn scooted closer to Colt. "I can keep her busy. You need to save your guy."

Colt nodded and put his hand on the table. The wood top was fake. Sol Levante's thoroughness was impressive. They were meticulous in their setup, leaving his team with no edge or advantage.

"Murph." Colt pointed to the window. "Vaughn, we could use a cushy landing."

Pulling the axe from his back holster, Murph raised the axe high above his head as he ran toward the window, chucking the axe a few feet before he reached it. The axe smashed into the window, shattering it. Murph dove after it, disappearing from view into the night.

Colt waved to Grace. "Time to go!" He leaped through the open window after Murph; a rush of excitement filled him, jumping into the unknown. Then a wall of air enveloped Colt, lowering him to the ground next to Murph.

"Was that an assassin?" Grace stepped down from the air cushion beside them.

Murph picked up his axe and brushed the glass off his jacket. "I've heard of a Renewing assassin named Jamie."

"I think she invited us to play volleyball at the beach," said Colt, thinking out loud.

What would the Renewing be doing here? They'd taken over most of Lunos, but that wasn't a problem on Earth. The Vigil were keeping a close eye on the situation, but so far, the Renewing hadn't done anything to warrant concern for the security of humanity.

Colt took one last look at the window they came through before leading his team to the temple. "We don't have time to worry about that now. We need to get to the temple and save Seamus."

THE TEMPLE OF SOL WAS HUNDREDS, IF NOT THOUSANDS, OF YEARS old, so the steps leading up to it should have been worn down from years of use and exposure to the elements. Instead, they looked like they had been freshly cut. Colt, Grace, and Murph pulled up their hoods as droplets of rain started to fall from the dark clouds above them.

A supernatural glow seemed to come from the Temple of Sol, shifting between a light purple to a deep blue color. The three of them remained silent as they ascended the stairs, no people or creatures stirring around them.

It wasn't until they got to the main temple grounds that they could hear the sounds of voices in the distance. Colt motioned for them to stay down.

"Stay together," he whispered. "We don't know what we're getting into."

Murph unstrapped the axe he had on his back, holding it at the ready. Grace slid one of her knifes out of her boot, taking the lead—he'd always been the stealthiest of the group.

When they got close enough, they could see Sol Levante acolytes gathered in a circle in the courtyard to the temple, torches all around them sizzling in the rain. Each of them wore the black robes with their hoods up. In the center of them was an altar, with an orb the size of a magic eight ball resting on a pillow. Mateo was in a form-fitting battle jacket with the hood up and his scythe next to him, his Shinigami armored gauntlet on his left hand. He was in his full Shinigami gear, seemingly protecting the orb.

Shinigami were the best trained and most loyal among the Vigil. If Mateo was prepared to kill other Vigil for Sol Levante, then Jorah had reason to be worried. This was worse than a rogue relic.

Orator Meg walked out in red robes, standing out in the sea of black, her arms high in the air. A hush fell over the crowd.

"Brothers, sisters, this is the time we've been waiting for. Finally, we have a descendant of the seven with us."

The crowd cheered as Seamus walked out of the temple, still wearing the blue gi he had on earlier.

Meg raised her hands in the air, silencing the crowd. "Through his blood, we come closer to walking in Sol's Fields of Light." She took a few steps closer to the orb and pulled out a decorative dagger, the handle gold and covered in gems.

"I think that's our cue," said Colt. Grace just looked at him. "What? I thought you said that you could take *any* Shinigami?"

Grace scoffed.

Murph scooted closer. "I was more concerned with the twenty-plus other acolytes and Meg. You saw what she did back in the city."

"She doesn't have the staff with her now. Without it, I doubt she's as powerful." Colt tried to sound confident. *I hope the staff was where all her power came from.*

"That still leaves twenty-two of them and three of us." Murph sounded uncharacteristically concerned.

Colt pulled some bark out of his pockets, which he'd collected on their way to the temple. He slid them under his sleeves, allowing them to fuse to his skin, creating small bracers. "Grace, how well can you get wet wood to burn?" He wiped some rain from his eyes.

"What does that have to do with anything?" she asked.

Straining against the pain as the bark fused, Colt pulled out his phone and set a timer for forty-five minutes, then pointed toward the jungle. "If we give them something else to worry about, that should leave less of them for us to handle." Closing his eyes, Colt focused on his breathing, using his Animancy to prepare his body. "Make it quick. Meg's long-winded, but I don't know how long we have."

Grace smiled in understanding, pulled out a lighter, and dropped behind a ruin wall, going toward the jungle.

"That makes twenty-two to *two*." Murph tightened his grip on his axe handle.

They inched closer to the courtyard again.

Orator Meg waved her hands in the air as she spoke. "Remember this day when you tell your children the tales of how you helped bring Sol's light to the people of Earth. It is unfortunate that Lux Dei Isom cannot be here with us today, but he is hard at work finding the descendants of the other seven to unlock the gate."

"She's really putting on a show," whispered Murph, looking between her and the jungle below.

Blinking a few times, Colt's eyes finally adjusted to the darkness through the trees. He could see the brief flickers of light in the jungle where Grace was making her preparations. "Grace'll have quite the show for them soon."

he started the timer on his phone. Fifty-three minutes was the longest he'd ever been able to use the full animal instinct technique. So, forty-five minutes would give him plenty of time.

"Seamus step forward. Lead us into the new day!" Meg held the dagger high in the air.

Colt inched closer to the courtyard, his stomach in knots. There was no waiting for a better time, no waiting for reinforcements. He wasn't going to lose another team member. Things would be different this time. If he'd been faster, just *acted*, Nicki wouldn't be lying comatose in a hospital bed. This time, he would act.

And after they saved Seamus, they could get Vigil reinforcements and get the staff from Meg to heal Nicki.

A dozen pillars of flame erupted in the jungle next to the temple, each of them thirty feet tall.

Mateo was the first into action, ready to run for the jungle.

"Mateo." Meg's voice was cold and clear. "You are needed here. We will continue. The rest of you find out what is happening. Put out the flames before they attract the demons here."

All but three acolytes ran down the stairs and into the jungle toward Grace's fire pillars.

Murph stood up straight. "Two on five. Now those odds I can work with."

"Usual bet?" asked Colt.

"Loser buys the first round."

Grace stomped up the hill beside them. "When I win, you both owe me a new dress. I ripped this one running around out there."

"*Three* on five." Murph helped Grace over the remains of a wall.

"And Seamus makes four." Colt took the lead, marching through the rain out into the open. "You won't be killing anyone today, Orator Meg!"

"It seems like you've made that decision for me." Orator Meg took a step back, letting her acolytes move between her and Colt.

Colt drew his sword. "Don't worry, Seamus, we're going to make sure that you get out of this just fine. You just have to trust us."

"No." Seamus grabbed the dagger out of Meg's hand.

"What are you doing?" she asked.

"None of you are going to take this moment from me. It's finally my time." Seamus used the dagger to cut open his palm. "This is the time for me to take my place above all of you, where I've always belonged."

Colt was stunned. How could Seamus do this? He'd invited him into their family.

"Sniveling Swabby," said Grace. I knew I was right about him." The flames in the torches rose with Grace's anger.

Mateo held his battle scythe toward them, calming the flames. "I don't want to hurt any of you. It isn't too late to put down your weapons and surrender."

Seamus groaned in frustration. "You will give me the respect I deserve. All of you." He slammed his bloody hand down on the orb.

The orb levitated in the air. A deep purple light began emanating from it, the same color as the glow the temple had earlier. Once the orb was about five feet in the air, it disappeared into a column of purple light stretching high into the sky, cutting through the storm. The light got darker where the orb had been, turning black. A stench of death and decay filled the area. Then a fog with a greenish tint to it began pouring out of the darkness, extending from where the orb was. The blackness continued to extend up and down the pillar of light, stretching from the ground to about twelve feet in the air, creating a fracture between worlds. Fog began gushing out like waves as the blackness extended, bouncing across the ground as it spread.

Dread overtook Colt. He hadn't noticed that he was reflexively taking steps backward. The feeling was stronger than anything he'd felt so far.

A wolf's snout protruded from the blackness, nine feet in the air. It sniffed deeply before continuing forward. The fur on the snout was a moss-green color, like the fog. It was shorter than a regular wolf and had large nostrils like a cow. Soon the creature's head was free of the fracture. The thick horns protruding from the bare skull between the creature's wolflike ears were by far its most prominent feature. The thick ram-like horns stretched and curved around the creature's face, coming to points near the end of the snout, providing additional protection for the creature's yellow eyes.

Long human fingers with claws gripped the edges of the fracture as the creature pulled itself free. Colt could see the same mossy fur on its barreled chest between the large bone plates that extended from the creature's spine around its body. The bone plates formed an outer exoskeleton for the creature, its inner ribcage visible under its skin as it continued to wriggle free of the fracture. Similar bone plates covered the biceps of the creature's muscular arms. Its digitigrade legs had bone plates from the hip to the knee.

The fracture between worlds flickered and closed as the creature pulled its bony tail free. Black ooze dripped from its large fangs. The orb dropped back down onto its cushion.

"Listen to me—your master!" said Seamus. "Kill those three. Show us your power." Seamus pointed to Colt, Grace, and Murph.

Colt didn't think the pain of betrayal could hurt more than it already had. He was wrong.

The creature turned its head toward Seamus and then slowly gazed over all the people present. It swung at the acolyte closest to it, effortlessly ripping him apart.

"Something's wrong." Meg said to Mateo and inched back. The creature gorged itself on the acolyte. "This should have worked. He should have control of the creature. I did everything right." She positioned herself behind Mateo. "*They* must be the problem. Slay the demon and the three Vigil: their dark presence corrupted the ritual." She grabbed Seamus's arm, pulling him toward the temple. Colt tried to follow but was forced away from the reach of Mateo's scythe.

Mateo swung his scythe around his head, pulling the flames from the torches, collecting them above him, creating a hulking ball of fire. Then he directed the fireball at the creature with the scythe.

The creature yelped as the flames crashed into it, its fur sizzling.

Grace and Murph looked back and forth between the creature and Colt, waiting for him to give them direction. He'd already really lost Seamus. He couldn't lose them too. "Fall back to the tree line." Colt leaped over the short stone wall ruins into some trees. They followed.

Mateo was swing his scythe at the creature, but it bounced off the bones, not even leaving a mark. He threw more flames at it. The creature shied away from the flames slightly. An acolyte leaped at the creature, trying to stab it with a dagger. It swung its arm, backhanding the acolyte effortlessly, tossing them into a wall.

Murph peered past a tree. "I've never seen or read of a creature like that before. Do you think it's a demon like Meg said?"

"Should we run while it's distracted?" asked Grace.

Colt's instincts screamed at him to run. To get away. To protect his team. His mind raced, studying the creature. Forward-facing eyes, sharp fangs, claws—all attributes that pointed to the creature being a predator. But the outer shell of bone and horns gave it the defensive feel of prey. A dangerous mix, creating a creature bred for destruction, a threat to humanity.

"Colt?" Murph shouted at him.

"No. We took an oath to defend humanity. We need to stop that creature before it gets to those who can't defend themselves."

The creature got down on all fours, keeping its head down against the flamethrower that Mateo was unleashing against it. Charging forward, the creature gored him with the horns on its head. The creature flung its head from side to side until Mateo slid off the horns and crashed to the ground.

The ground shook as the creature tramped after the last acolyte; it snapped a deep bite at the base of the acolyte's neck. His screams filled the night air until there was a loud crunch, followed by silence.

"How do you plan on stopping that thing?" asked Grace, her entire body was trembling.

"That thing took out a Shinigami, taking no noticeable injuries," agreed Murph. "I think we're a little out of our league, Colt." Murph was trying to act brave, but Colt could see his white knuckles from gripping his axe so tightly. "I need to think." Colt closed his eyes, tuning out their words, and started running through his observations.

It killed a Shinigami, but that just meant they needed to be smart in their approach. He pushed the fear for his team down deep inside.

This creature was primarily a predator that was ripped away from everything it knew. *That's why it's lashing out at everything. It's lost and confused. Its general body build doesn't look like it has a high fat content. So, it doesn't look like it's built for something like swimming,*

"I have an idea. But neither of you are going to like it."

"You're really selling this." Grace peered around the tree she was hiding behind, watching the creature continue to gorge itself on the acolytes.

Murph nodded at him.

"I don't think it would be able to swim." Colt's voice trailed off as he continued to formulate his thoughts.

Grace let out a dry laugh. "That's all you've got? You're right, I don't like it."

Colt gave her a look. "I wasn't done yet. That wasn't the bad part. It doesn't look like it likes fire either, and we need to distract it."

"If we survive this, we need to talk about this recent trend of using me as a distraction. Murph is so much bigger and more noticeable than me."

"*Hey!* . . . Well, yeah." Murph reluctantly shrugged his shoulders.

""Are you both done? Like I was saying, we need to lure it to the cliff side overlooking the ocean and goad it into charging, then get it to charge off the edge and into the ocean."

Grace pointed to the far side of the courtyard. "How am I supposed to get past that thing and to the edge of the cliff? We're on the wrong side."

"Murph and I will have to get its attention first and then lead it to you. It's learned that charging into the flames works. We can use that to guide it over the edge." Colt looked at his phone. Twenty-eight minutes left. "If it gets too close to any one of us, we have to change its focus to someone else. I'll go first. As soon as you see an opening, Grace, run."

She let out a puff of air. "Ready," she replied.

"Murph?"

He nodded in reply.

"Stay sharp and don't take unnecessary risks." Colt heard the hypocrisy in his words as he ran directly toward the creature.

He caused a root to grow out of the ground ahead of him in the shape of a spear. Then Colt broke it free and threw it as hard as he could at the creature. It bounced off its outer bones. The creature continued to eat as though nothing had happened.

"I'll get your attention," he murmured. Colt kneeled, gently placing his hand on the ground. Thinking about the foul odor of the mist that came with the creature, he focused on the ground growing mint. As it grew, he weaved it into a tight ball.

Plucking the mint-ball out of the ground, Colt took careful aim at the creature's nose. The mint flew, small mounds of dirt falling from it, then burst on the creature's face. The creature reared up on its hind legs, snorting and clawing at its face.

Its yellow eyes narrowed in on Colt.

OK. That worked a little too well. Colt started running, jumping over and through the large stone remains of the temple grounds. The creature wasn't fast, but it tore through the stones, breaking them to pieces as it trudged through.

Colt could feel pebbles rattling against the back of his head. With each stone the creature shattered, the larger the pieces that hit Colt became. "Murph!" He could hear the panic setting in his own voice.

He glanced back to see a large rock crash against the creature's head, breaking against its horn. The next rock cracked against its exposed neck. The creature huffed, turning its head to chase Murph.

"Grace? You ready?" Colt yelled toward the cliff. A slight flash of flame puffed in the darkness. "I'll take that as a yes."

Murph did his best to raise walls between the creature and himself. None of them slowed it down. Apparently, once something or someone caught the creature's attention, it was like nothing else mattered. A few blasts of fire flew toward the creature, all of them fizzling out before they reached it. *She's too far away.*

Colt drew his sword. Not that he thought it would do any good, but it was the best that he had. He could see that the bone plates didn't cover the creature's entire leg. Sprinting toward it head on, Colt took his sword in a reverse grip to have a more powerful stab. He started a stabbing motion with both hands as he passed Murph.

The momentum drove the sword deep into the leg, tearing the sword out of Colt's hands and tripping the creature. He stumbled, waving his hands in the air to maintain his balance. The creature swiped at him. Colt blocked with his forearms together. There was a hollow sound as it smashed against his wood bracers. Then they buckled and cracked, breaking away. Colt used all his strength to hold his position as the creature fell forward. If it wasn't for his powers, the strike would have broken most of the bones in his body.

Scratching at the ground, the creature clambered back onto all fours. Then it lowered its head and charged Colt, flinging hunks of dirt behind it.

Focusing all his magical energy into his legs, Colt focused on the power and dexterity he'd learned from a horse. The muscles in his legs tensed and tightened before erupting with power, propelling Colt forward. All he could do was run, but he turned toward where Grace was. He could feel tiny tremors in the ground from the creature pounding behind him. An orange light filled his vision. He fell back, sliding on the ground, and then threw his weight to the side to roll out of the way.

The creature bellowed in pain against the flames that suddenly shot up at it, then doubled down on its charge. The plan was working. Grace stood out on the edge of the cliff, then dove out of the way moments before the creature's horns would have caught her. It dug its heels and claws into the soil, ripping it out, trying to stop before going over the edge.

Colt's heart dropped when the creature slowed to a stop, inches from the edge of the cliff. It stood up again, pulling the sword out of its leg and throwing it away.

If he could run fast and hard enough, maybe he could tackle it over the edge.

Colt ran toward the creature. After a few steps, he could feel his strength leaving him. He looked at his watch: time up. He'd overexerted himself. *No, no, no, no, not now. I just need a little more.* But falling to his knees, he knew there wasn't any more he could do. The way the creature exposed its teeth made it look like it was smiling.

The ground trembled beneath the creature, then it cracked, falling apart. It yelped, a high fear-filled sound, clawing for anything to secure itself. With one last yelp, it fell to the water below, the ocean's waves swallowing it whole.

Murph stood panting, both of his hands pointed at where the edge of the cliff had been. He beamed with joy as he lowered his hands.

Grace ran over to him, giving him a hug. "You did it!" she squealed, jumping up and down.

Colt laughed, forcing himself back to his feet. "Great job. Both of you. We did it."

"I'm impressed." A man's deep voice interrupted their celebration, followed by a loud, metallic slow clap. They turned: walking toward them was a bald man taller than Murph, in all black armor, a forest-green cape draped behind him. He carried a large war hammer on his back. It looked big enough that a normal person wouldn't be able to lift it, let alone swing it.

"Who are you?" asked Colt.

"Someone who is not easily impressed. Killing a Tirgel-heva is no easy feat." A handful of soldiers wearing similar armor walked into view behind him. "I'm Captain Thomas Miner. I wasn't expecting much resistance from the Vigil, but if there are others like you among their ranks, we might have a proper fight ahead of us."

"So that's it then. Sol Levante wants to eliminate the Vigil." Just one more thing confirming that his bad feeling about them was justified. "We won't let you."

Miner let out a hearty laugh. "Oh, that was good. Funny. Sol Levante is insignificant compared to the might of the Renewing. I admire your loyalty to the Vigil, but I think you'll find that they don't share it." He turned to one of his soldiers. "Contact Prime Jared and have him add these three to the Vigil's wanted list. Mark them as traitors. It shouldn't be hard to do with a dead Shinigami."

"We had nothing to do with Mateo's death." Grace's fury came through her words.

Colt stumbled his way back to Grace and Murph.

"I know you didn't. All I'm trying to do is help you understand the options that you have. Escaping and going back to the Vigil isn't one of them." Miner had a stern, but smug look on his face as he spoke.

The girl from the beach stepped out into the open. She was wearing a red leather jacket with blue jeans. The bow in her hand had an arrow nocked. "What do you want me to do with them?"

Colt felt the fear erupting inside of him, had the Renewing been following them this entire time? All the Vigil reports said the Renewing was on operating on Lunos, and they hadn't brought any operations to Earth.

"We're on a time crunch to get this orb moving . . ."

Cutting Miner off, Meg proudly walked out of the jungle, her forearms a blaze the fire making her a beacon in the dark. "I can handle things from here. We don't need the Renewing edging in on our operations."

Miner folded his arms looking down at Meg. "Tell Isom to keep his house in order and we won't need to come next time. Try and bring those three on as assets. If not, Jamie, you know what to do. My men will secure the orb and clear out the jungle."

"I guess I was right. We did have a chance to play together." Jamie sounded playful, keeping her bow at the ready. "Choices time. Are you going to make this easy and come with me, or do I get to have some fun?"

"Excuse me." Meg nudged Jamie with her shoulder forcing her way past.

Jamie looked daggers at Meg. Miner shook his head at Jamie folding his arms. "She's made her bed, let her lie in it." He turned around and walked back toward the jungle.

Even with all the time they were wasting fighting amongst themselves, Colt still couldn't see a way out. The only two options were surrender or death. Either way he'd failed his team.

Meg cleared her throat taking back the spotlight. "Make the right choice Colt. There is still time for you to come back to the Sanctuary and join Seamus."

"I may have failed my team, but I haven't failed myself." Standing up straight, Colt put his left fist over his heart. "Humanity's shield against the night."

"We are the Vigil." Grace and Murph said in sync.

"Have it your way." Jamie pulled the string back on her bow.

A gale of wind threw Colt, Grace, and Murph off the edge of the cliff.

"Too slow," echoed Vaughn's voice. He flew over the edge, diving toward them. "We've got some work to do." An air bubble surrounded them all, padding their fall, as they sank into the ocean.

Colt looked around at what was left of his team, cushioned in the bubble of air. Things hadn't gone the way they'd expected, but now he knew there was a staff that could heal Nicki. Seamus chose another path, but Grace and Murph were still at his side. They were alive and free. That meant they had hope. Together they could stop Meg and save Nicki.

THE END